Learning to Read and Write
Step by Step!

Ready to Read and Write Preschool–Kindergarten
• big type and easy words
• picture clues
• drawing and first writing activities

For children who like to "tell" stories by drawing pictures and are eager to write.

Reading and Writing with Help Preschool–Grade 1
• basic vocabulary
• short sentences
• simple writing activities

For children who use letters, words, and pictures to tell stories.

Reading and Writing on Your Own Grades 1–3
• popular topics
• easy-to-follow plots
• creative writing activities

For children who are comfortable writing simple sentences on their own.

STEP INTO READING® Write-In Readers are designed to give every child a successful reading and writing experience. The grade levels are only guides. Children can progress through the steps at their own speed, developing confidence in their abilities, no matter what grade.

Remember, a lifetime love of reading and writing starts with a single step!

Thomas the Tank Engine & Friends®

A BRITT ALLCROFT COMPANY PRODUCTION

Based on The Railway Series by The Reverend W Awdry
© 2004 Gullane (Thomas) LLC
Thomas the Tank Engine & Friends and Thomas & Friends are trademarks
of Gullane Entertainment Inc.
Thomas the Tank Engine & Friends is Reg. U.S. Pat. TM Off.

A HIT Entertainment Company

All rights reserved under International and Pan-American Copyright Conventions.
Published in the United States by Random House Children's Books, a division of
Random House, Inc., New York, and simultaneously in Canada by Random House
of Canada Limited, Toronto.

www.stepintoreading.com

www.thomasthetankengine.com

Educators and librarians, for a variety of teaching tools, visit us at
www.randomhouse.com/teachers

Library of Congress Control Number: 2003114588
ISBN: 0-375-82892-3

Printed in the United States of America
First Edition 10 9 8 7 6

STEP INTO READING, RANDOM HOUSE, and the Random House colophon are registered
trademarks of Random House, Inc.

Thomas Comes to Breakfast

A Write-In Reader

Illustrated by Richard Courtney and

_____

your name

Random House 🏠 New York

It is morning.

5

Thomas wants to
drive on his own.

What can you do on your own?

Draw a picture of yourself doing it.

Thomas starts to go.

He can not stop.

Will the buffers stop him?

Circle things that make you stop.

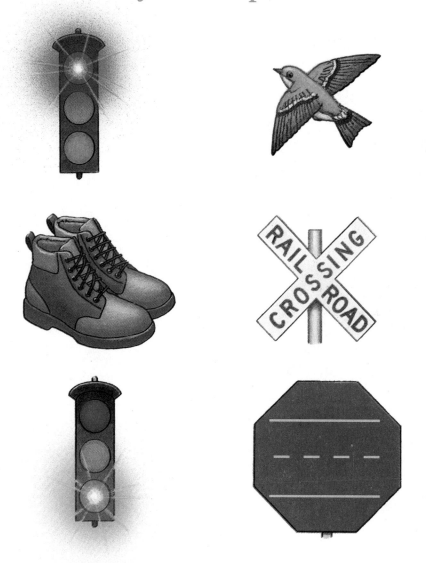

Write STOP in the stop sign.

Oh, no!

CRASH!

Look out for the house!

STATIONMASTER

A family is
eating breakfast.

What do you like to eat?
Draw it.

Thomas can not stop.

Oh, no!

CRASH!

17

Who crashed into the wall?

Thomas did!

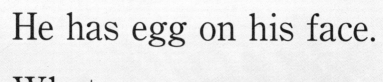

He has egg on his face.

What a mess.

19

The family is mad.

Draw a mad face.

Thomas is sad.

Draw a sad face.

Thomas must wait
for Donald and Douglas.

Donald and Douglas look alike. Connect the pictures that look alike.

Donald and Douglas
pull Thomas free.

Thomas looks silly.
Donald and Douglas
laugh at him.

Workmen fix Thomas.

cap

ladder

man

ramp

28

Finish the names
of things you see
in this picture.

_ _ _ _ ap

_ _ _ _ adder

_ _ _ _ an

_ _ _ _ amp

Thomas has learned

not to drive on his own . . .

until next time.